THOMAS & FRIENDS

BLUE MOUNTAIN MYSTERY

Illustrated by Tommy Stubbs

A GOLDEN BOOK · NEW YORK

Thomas the Tank Engine & Friends™

CREATED BY BRITT ALLCROFT

Based on The Railway Series by The Reverend W Awdry.
© 2012 Gullane (Thomas) LLC.
HIT and the HIT Entertainment logo are trademarks of HIT Entertainment Limited.
All rights reserved. Published in the United States by Golden Books, an imprint of Random House Children's Books, a division of Random House, Inc., 1745 Broadway, New York, NY 10019, and in Canada by Random House of Canada Limited, Toronto.
Golden Books, A Golden Book, A Big Golden Book, the G colophon, and the distinctive gold spine are registered trademarks of Random House, Inc.
randomhouse.com/kids   www.thomasandfriends.com
ISBN: 978-0-307-93149-8
Printed in the United States of America
10 9 8 7 6 5 4 3 2
Random House Children's Books supports the First Amendment and celebrates the right to read.

It was a busy day at the Blue Mountain Quarry. Rusty shunted trucks of slate. Owen moved equipment up and down the rocky walls. Because of the steep hills and tight turns at the quarry, the engines that worked there were smaller and lighter than other engines. They had special tracks and were called Narrow Gauge engines.

Paxton, a visiting Diesel, was impressed by how hard all the Narrow Gauge engines worked.

"If your wheels aren't whirring," said Skarloey, "you're not being Really Useful!"

Suddenly, there was a loud noise. Giant stones were falling from Blondin Bridge!

"Fenders and fireboxes!" shouted Peter Sam. "The bridge isn't safe! No one must cross it!"

At that moment, Rheneas was rolling down from the Upper Terrace. He tried to stop, but his heavy trucks pushed him toward the dangerous bridge. He sped up so he could race across the bridge before it collapsed.

Rheneas made it! The bridge thundered apart behind him as he skidded to a stop at the bottom of the hill. Everyone was relieved that the danger was over.

Then they saw poor Paxton. He was buried under some fallen stones. He was all right, but he was definitely in need of repairs.

Thomas was working hard with Annie and Clarabel when Sir Topham Hatt drove up in Winston the track car.

"Thomas, I have a special job for you," said Sir Topham Hatt. "Paxton has been in an accident and must go to the Dieselworks for repairs. I need you to work at the quarry in his place."

Thomas beamed from buffer to buffer. "I like working with my Narrow Gauge friends," he whistled.

Thomas quickly chugged to the Blue Mountain Quarry.
The Narrow Gauge engines were happy to see him, and blew
their whistles in welcome.

"Hello, my friends!" peeped Thomas. "I'm ready to huff my
hardest! Just tell me what I need to do!"

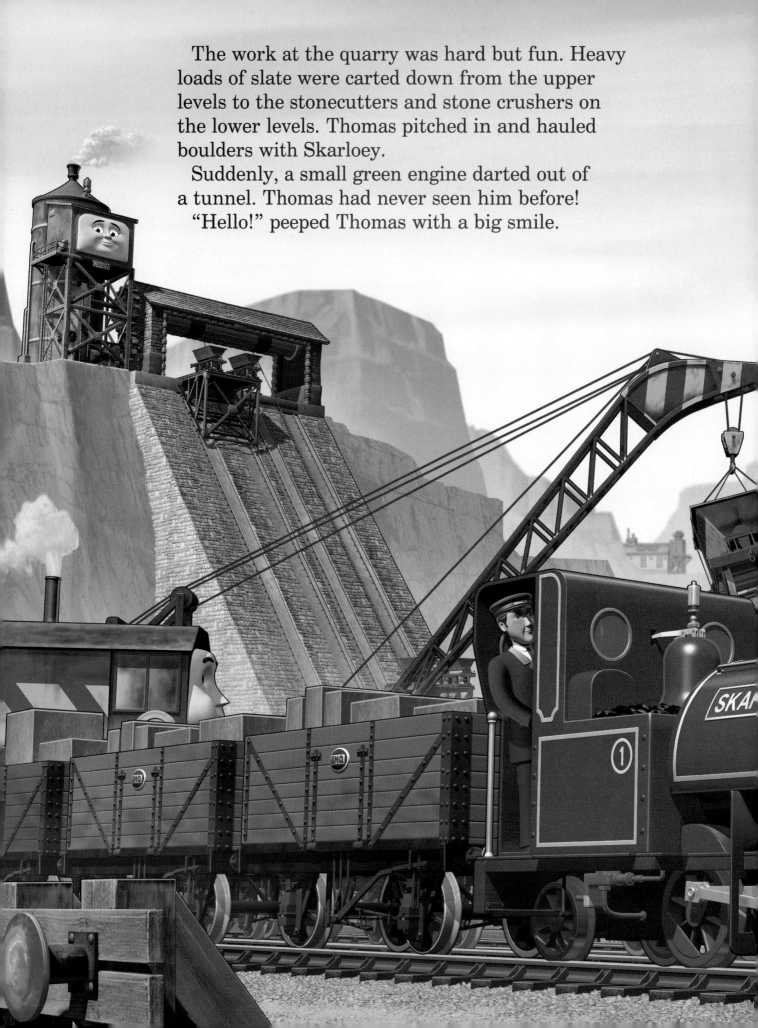

The work at the quarry was hard but fun. Heavy loads of slate were carted down from the upper levels to the stonecutters and stone crushers on the lower levels. Thomas pitched in and hauled boulders with Skarloey.

Suddenly, a small green engine darted out of a tunnel. Thomas had never seen him before!

"Hello!" peeped Thomas with a big smile.

But the little green engine didn't answer. He quickly rolled into another tunnel.

"Cinders and ashes!" whistled Thomas. "How strange! I wonder who that little green engine is."

Later, Thomas asked Rusty about the little green engine. Rusty was quiet for a moment, then finally answered. "I think . . . I'm pretty sure . . . it was a mountain goat."

"It wasn't a mountain goat," peeped Thomas. "It was an engine."

The next morning as Thomas puffed to the quarry, he saw the little green engine again.

"Who are you?" Thomas asked. Without saying a word, the green engine puffed off. Thomas sped after him.

"Go, Luke!" cried Skarloey as he and the other Narrow Gauge engines rolled into position to block Thomas.

"Skarloey!" huffed Thomas. "Who is Luke? Why does he keep puffing away? Why will none of you talk to me about him?"

"Thomas, you are our friend," said Skarloey, "so we trust you." The other engines whistled in agreement.

"Luke hides here at the Blue Mountain Quarry because he is scared," Skarloey said. "Once, long ago, Luke did something very bad. He thinks if anyone finds him, he will be sent away from Sodor forever. That's why we make sure he always stays hidden."

Thomas promised to keep the secret locked in his funnel.

When Thomas had finished working that night, he decided he needed some time to think. So he steamed to a quiet hill by himself.

"What did Luke do that was so bad?" Thomas wondered aloud. "Don't worry, Luke, I'll find a way to help you."

But Thomas wasn't really alone. Someone was watching—and hoping that Thomas *could* find a way to help.

The next morning as Thomas chuffed to work, Luke
appeared by his side.

"Hi, Thomas," he said. "I'm sorry I hid from you. I didn't
know you, but now I wonder . . . will you be my friend?"

"I'd like that, Luke," said Thomas. "I'd like that very much."

Thomas and Luke worked together at the boulder drop all day. Luke dropped giant rocks down the chute, and Thomas collected the broken gravel at the bottom.

Suddenly, a horn honked. Winston had arrived, carrying Sir Topham Hatt and Mr. Percival, the controller of the Narrow Gauge Railway. Luke quickly hid.

"Thank you for your work, Thomas," said Mr. Percival. "Paxton will now take over again."

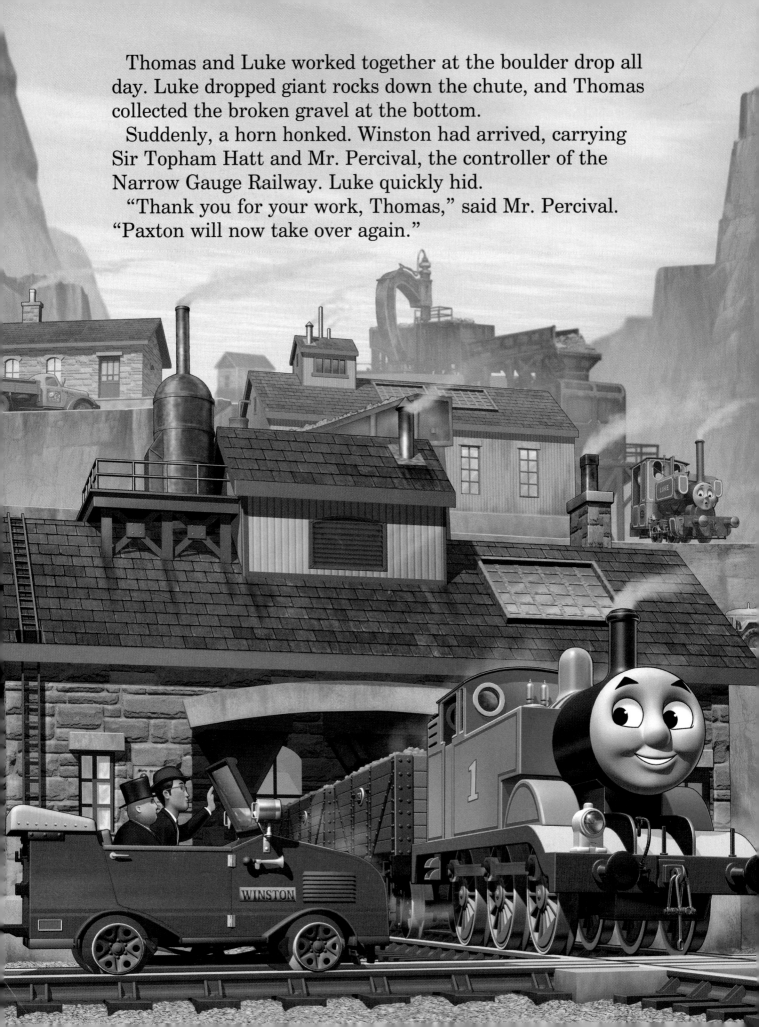

When Winston had motored away, Thomas asked Luke why he felt he had to hide.

"I did something very bad," said Luke.

"I've done bad things, too," peeped Thomas. "Once, I steamed right past a Danger sign and fell into a mine! And I'm still here."

Luke giggled. The two new friends were so busy talking that they didn't hear Paxton puff up behind them. Paxton listened quietly as Luke told his story.

"I first came to the Island of Sodor on a boat," said Luke. "Next to me was a little yellow engine. He was chained to the deck like I was. He had come from far away.

"A storm blew in, and the ship was tossed around on the waves. My chains rattled something fierce. The little yellow engine was scared. He spoke a strange language I didn't understand. I wanted to reassure him, but I didn't know how.

"We finally reached Sodor, but the little yellow engine still looked scared. The dockworkers wanted to lift him off right away, but I pleaded to be first. They agreed, and I was happy!

"But then I bumped into the little yellow engine . . . and sent him splashing into the sea!"

Paxton couldn't believe what he had heard. He raced off to tell Diesel.

An idea flew into Thomas' funnel. "I know what I'll do!" said Thomas. "I'll find out what happened to that little yellow engine. Maybe he's at the Dieselworks!"

Thomas reached the Dieselworks just as Paxton finished
telling Diesel the story. Thomas was shocked. No one else
was supposed to know about Luke and the little yellow engine.
"We have to tell Sir Topham Hatt and Mr. Percival,"
said Diesel. "They'll make Luke leave forever!"
Thomas was worried. He had to find that little yellow engine
before Diesel could get Luke in trouble.

Thomas chuffed to the Steamworks, where Victor was hard
at work.

"Victor, do you remember fixing a little yellow engine
that fell into the sea?" Thomas asked.

Victor stopped working immediately. His eyes were wide
with surprise. Thomas suddenly understood.

"Cinders and ashes!" whistled Thomas. "*You* were the engine that fell into the sea!"

"You are right, Thomas," said Victor. "It was me."

Victor's story about his trip to the Island of Sodor was the same as Luke's—except for one important detail.

"During the storm, a big wave broke the chains holding my wheels," Victor said. "Nothing held me to the deck! I called to the crew, but they didn't understand me. No one could help me.

"I barely made it to the dock," Victor went on. "And when they lifted the excited green engine, he swayed and bumped into me. I slid into the sea because there were no chains to stop me. When Cranky finally fished me out, I was in a terrible state."

"So it was all an accident!" peeped Thomas. "And you were repaired!"

"Yes," replied Victor. "I chose to be painted red—a bright new color for my bright new life!"

"I have to tell Luke!" said Thomas.

"Is Luke the little green engine?" asked Victor.

"Yes," said Thomas. "And he needs your help."

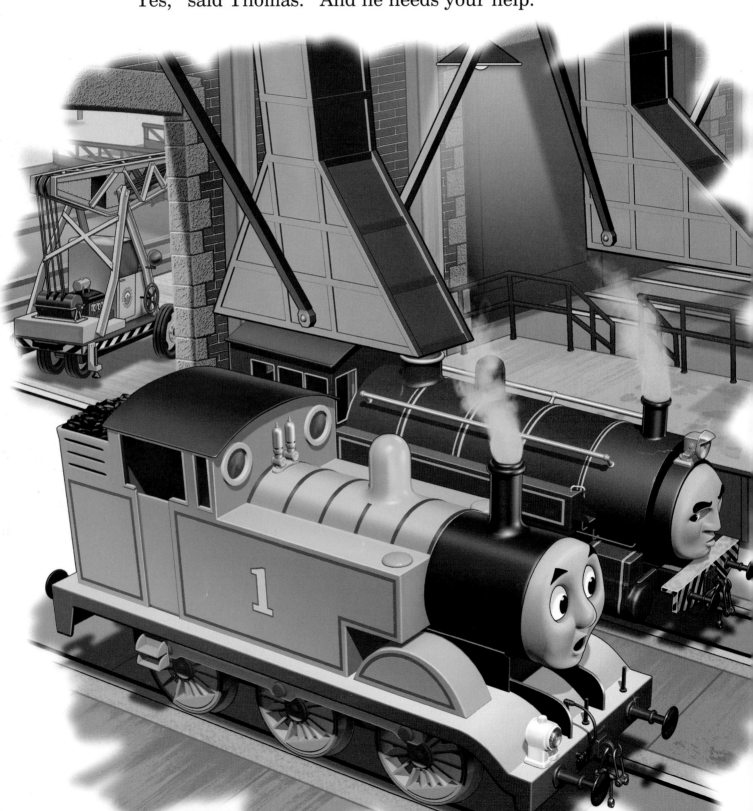

Later that day, Diesel and Paxton found Luke at the Blue Mountain Quarry. Luke rolled up the narrow gauge tracks, where Thomas, Diesel, and Paxton's standard gauge wheels couldn't follow.

"You can run, but you can't hide!" shouted Diesel. "Sir Topham Hatt is on his way! He's going to kick you off Sodor! Thomas can't save you now!"

"Yes, I can!" peeped Thomas as he sped into the quarry.

The Narrow Gauge engines were mad because they thought Thomas had revealed Luke's secret. Thomas didn't have time to explain.

"Rocky, please lift me onto Owen's platform. I have to talk to Luke!"

"Hold on tight!" shouted Rocky, and he hoisted Thomas up as high as he could—but it wasn't high enough.

Thomas needed Owen's help to climb higher up the quarry's rocky walls. Owen was nervous about lifting the heavy engine.

With a creak and a grunt, Owen's platform started to rise. Thomas went higher and higher until he reached the top of the incline.

"Upper Terrace!" shouted Owen. "Boulder drop and Blondin Bridge!"

"Well done!" Thomas peeped. But there was a problem. . . .

Thomas' wheels were too big for the narrow gauge tracks! They skidded and slid and jumped off the rails. Thomas rolled toward the edge of the cliff.

"Help!" Thomas peeped.

Just then, Luke came around a bend.

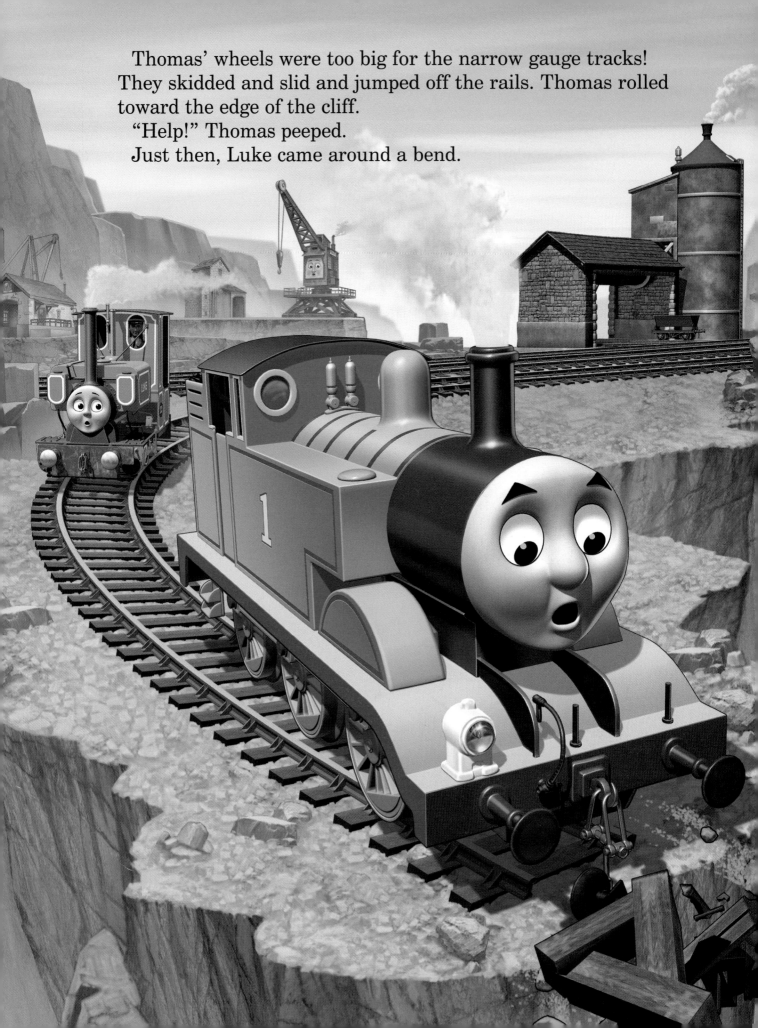

"Watch out, Thomas!" cried Diesel. "He's going to push you off! Just like he did to that yellow engine!"

Everyone waited. They watched as Luke slowly rolled toward Thomas.

"Don't worry, Thomas," said Luke. "I'll pull you back to Owen."

Luke buffered gently up to Thomas and slowly but surely pulled him back toward the platform.

"You're doing it, Luke!" whistled Thomas. Luke felt stronger than he had ever felt before.

Luke got Thomas safely to Owen's platform, but the weight of the two engines together was too much for Owen. The platform began to drop straight down.

"Whoa!" cried Luke.

"Cinders and ashes!" shouted Thomas.

"You're too heavy!" Owen grunted as he tried to slow the platform.

Owen strained and struggled and worked his hardest. Gears whined. Sparks flew. Owen stopped the platform before it hit the ground. Thomas and Luke were safe! The engines all whistled and cheered, except for Diesel, who scowled.

Just then, Sir Topham Hatt and Mr. Percival arrived. They were confused and more than a little angry.

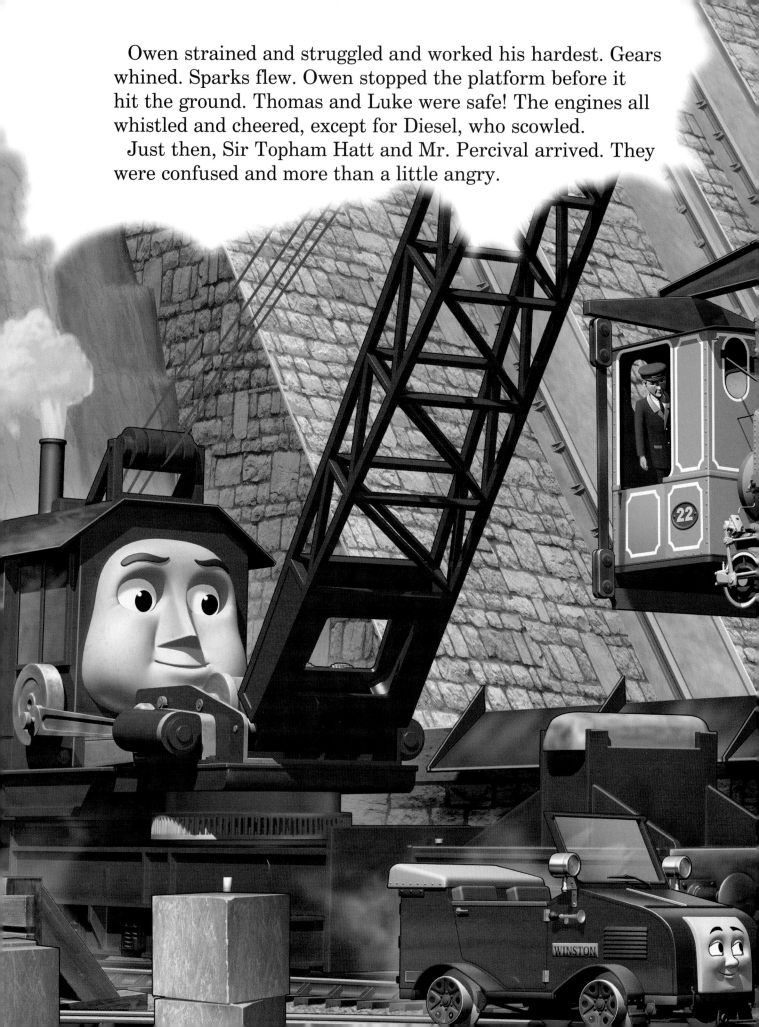

"Thomas, what are you doing here?" asked Sir Topham Hatt. "Rocky, bring those engines down from the unloading platform."

Little Luke was scared. Everyone held their breath.

"That engine up there is called Luke!" said Diesel. "He's a bad engine. He pushed a yellow engine into the sea. Thomas has been hiding him up here."

"It's not like that at all, sir," Thomas peeped. "I can explain!" But Thomas didn't have to say another word.

Victor steamed into the quarry. Everyone was very surprised to see him.

"I have come here to meet an engine I have not seen in a very long time," Victor puffed. "His name is Luke."

Rocky set Luke down. The little green engine was scared.

"Luke, you didn't push me," Victor said. "I slipped off. My wheel chains had broken. It was an accident."

"But it can't be you. You're not a yellow engine," Luke said.
"I was yellow," Victor explained, "but I was painted red when Sir Topham Hatt had me repaired. You should come down and visit me at the Steamworks. You can also get a coat of paint and a polish, and you will be a new engine, too!"
Luke laughed. For the first time in a long, long time, he was truly happy.

Sir Topham Hatt was very upset with Diesel. "You didn't find out the whole story before you caused confusion and delay," he said. "It's always important to find out what really happened. Because what really happened is what really matters."

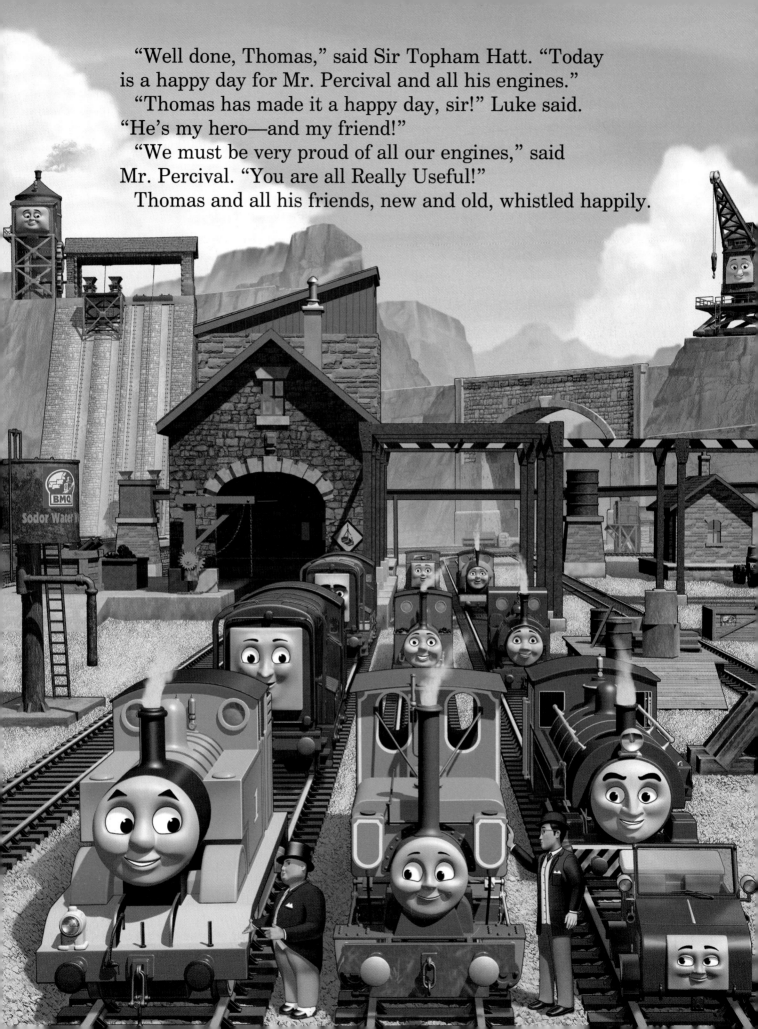

"Well done, Thomas," said Sir Topham Hatt. "Today is a happy day for Mr. Percival and all his engines."

"Thomas has made it a happy day, sir!" Luke said. "He's my hero—and my friend!"

"We must be very proud of all our engines," said Mr. Percival. "You are all Really Useful!"

Thomas and all his friends, new and old, whistled happily.

In the early 1940s, a loving father crafted a small blue wooden engine for his son, Christopher. The stories that this father, the Reverend W Awdry, made up to accompany the wonderful toy were first published in 1945. Reverend Awdry continued to create new adventures and characters until 1972, when he retired from writing.

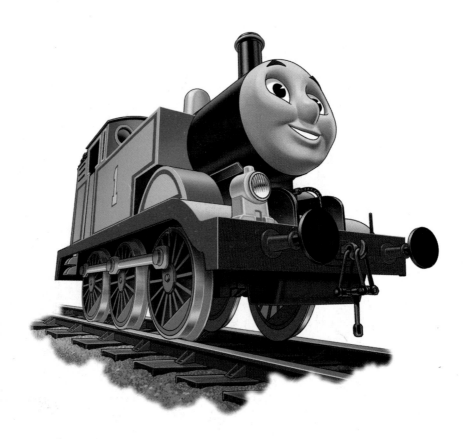

Tommy Stubbs has been an illustrator for several decades. Lately, he has been illustrating the newest tales of Thomas and his engine friends, including *May the Best Engine Win!*, *Thomas and the Great Discovery*, *Hero of the Rails*, *Misty Island Rescue*, and *Day of the Diesels*.